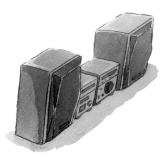

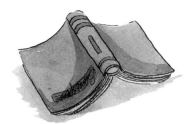

Jack's First Crush
傑克的戀愛初體驗

Coleen Reddy　著

倪靖、郜欣、王平　繪

蘇秋華　譯

三民書局

For Lyn and Sharlene

Two Extraordinary Sisters

獻給我特別的姊妹們——Lyn及Sharlene

Jack Smith was fifteen years old. He and his sister, Amy, went to Dogooder Junior High School. Jack did not like school and he was very afraid of the principal, Mr. Stern. Mr. Stern was always yelling at him and scolding him for some reason.

1

But recently, Jack looked forward to school. In fact, instead of always being late, he started going early to school. His family wondered what had gotten into him.

He also began dressing differently. Usually Jack was scruffy and looked untidy. But now he was wearing clean clothes and started using gel on his hair. He even used his father's aftershave. His parents were happy about the new Jack but they could not help wondering why he had suddenly changed. Amy thought Jack was weird, and weird people did weird things. But even she smelled something fishy.

4

One night, Amy was walking past the living room when she saw something strange. Jack was using the telephone but he wasn't talking to anyone. He would dial a number and then slam the telephone down a few seconds later. Once, he looked like he really wanted to say something. His mouth opened and he was trying to speak, but no sounds came out his mouth. Eventually, he put the phone down. This happened about five times. Amy was dying of curiosity.

"What are you doing?" Amy asked her brother.

Jack jumped up and screamed.

"You scared me! I didn't know you were here," Jack said.

"Well, who were you trying to phone?" asked Amy.

"No one. I was just testing the phone," Jack said, nervously.

"Testing the phone?" asked Amy, with a look of disbelief.

"Um, um, yes. I just wanted to see if it was working," said Jack.

"You're lying. I saw you. You were calling someone and then hanging up. Are you playing pranks on people?" asked Amy.

"No! I told you that I was testing the phone. Anyway, it's NOYB," yelled Jack.

"NOYB?" asked Amy.

"Yeah, None Of Your Business!" said Jack and he walked out of the room.

Amy shook her head. Jack was getting weirder every day.

A few days later, Amy was doing the laundry. She hated doing chores, but if she didn't do them, her parents wouldn't give her an allowance. She picked up Jack's smelly pants and something fell out of them.

It looked like a letter that Jack had written. Amy wondered whether she should read it. It was rude to read other people's letters, but in the end her curiosity got the better of her. It wasn't just any letter; it was a love letter. Amy read:

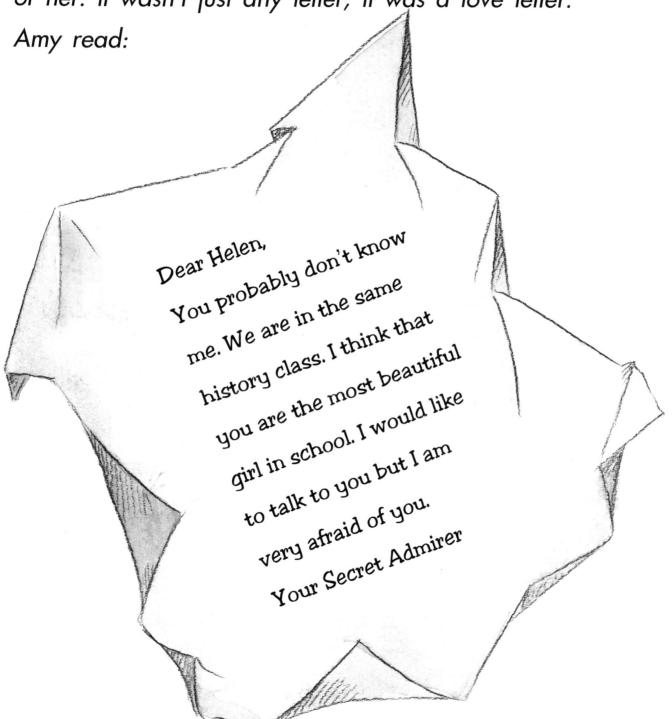

Dear Helen,
You probably don't know me. We are in the same history class. I think that you are the most beautiful girl in school. I would like to talk to you but I am very afraid of you.
Your Secret Admirer

"So that's what's going on with Jack. He's in love." Amy giggled. The idea of Jack being in love or having a girlfriend was very funny.

"I wonder who Helen is?" thought Amy.

The next day at school, Amy found out that Helen was really Helen Stern. She was the principal's daughter. That's why Jack was afraid; Mr. Stern didn't like Jack because he was always in trouble. Helen was very smart and kind of pretty. She was certainly not the prettiest girl in school. Love must be blind because Jack thought she was the prettiest girl.

Amy decided to talk to her brother. She might be able to help him.

That night she knocked on his bedroom door.

"Come in," Jack said. Amy walked in.

"What do you want?" he asked.

"Don't be rude. I only want to help you. I know you have a crush on Helen Stern," said Amy.

"What! Are you crazy? I don't know what you're talking about," yelled Jack.

"I found the letter you wrote to her," said Amy.

Jack was quiet. After a while he said, "Okay, so what if I have a crush on her?"

"You need help. I know you're scared. You know nothing about girls, so I can give you some advice," said Amy.

"You're right. I am afraid of her and her father. The other night, I tried calling her but every time she answered the phone, I got so nervous that I couldn't speak," Jack said.

"Maybe she's also scared. You should talk to her. I found out that she likes classical music and Shakespeare. You can talk to her about that," said Amy.

"I don't know anything about classical music or Shakespeare. It's useless. She'll never like someone as stupid as me," said Jack.

"People don't always want to date their twin. Maybe she'll find your stupidity charming," laughed Amy.

Jack picked up a pillow and started hitting Amy with it.

"Okay, okay. Look, you should try to talk to her. The worst that could happen is that she'll think you're a jerk and ignore you," said Amy.

Amy was right. Jack decided he would try. He knew that Helen spent a lot of time in the library. He took out a few Shakespeare plays from the library and borrowed his mother's classical CDs.

Jack saw Helen studying in the library. He sat down at a desk next to her. Then he put the Shakespeare plays on the desk so that Helen could easily see them. He pretended to be studying very hard.

After a while, Helen spoke to him.

"Hi," she said. "I noticed you were reading Shakespeare. Do you enjoy reading his plays?" asked Helen.

"Oh, yeah. I love them. I read them all the time," lied Jack.

"What's your favorite play?" asked Helen.

"Um, the one about those two lovers that die," said Jack.

"You mean 'Romeo and Juliet,'" said Helen.

"Yes, that's the one. It's so sad that they get murdered," said Jack.

"But they don't get murdered. They kill themselves," said Helen.

"That's what I meant," said Jack.

Helen went back to studying.

His plan hadn't worked. It was time for Plan B.

He picked up his bag and the CDs fell out.

"You listen to Bach and Mozart. Me too," said Helen.
"Yes, it's the only kind of music I listen to. I hate pop
music," said Jack. The truth was that Jack only listened to
pop music. He loved it.

"I like pop music a little. What about Puccini?" asked Helen.

"Yes, I love to eat pasta," said Jack.

Helen burst out laughing. Other people turned around and stared at them.

"Did I say something funny?" asked Jack.

"Puccini is not pasta; he is a famous composer. You're thinking of fettuccini, which is a kind of pasta," said Helen. She could not stop laughing.

"I knew that," said Jack. His plan had failed. It was all over. His true love thought he was the biggest idiot in the universe.

"You don't really listen to classical music, do you? I don't think you know much about Shakespeare either," said Helen.

But she wasn't angry; in fact she was smiling.

"No," said Jack, "I was just trying to impress you so that you'll like me. I'm sorry. I'll go now." Jack got up to leave.

"No, don't go. Maybe we can talk about something else," said Helen.

"Like what?" asked Jack.

"You can tell me about all the times you've been in trouble with my dad," said Helen.

"Why do you want to hear about that?" asked Jack.

"I'm sure that your stories will be pretty funny. I think you're pretty funny," said Helen, a little shyly.

That's how Jack and Helen had their first conversation. Amy, who had been watching everything from a distance, smiled. It looked like Helen was going to be Jack's first girlfriend.

傑克的戀愛初體驗

傑克・史密斯今年十五歲，他和妹妹愛玫都在督顧德國中唸書。傑克不喜歡上學，而且他很怕校長嚴先生。嚴校長總是對他大吼大叫，或找出各種理由嘲弄他。不過最近傑克卻變得很愛上學。以前總是遲到的他，現在居然天天早到。他的家人很好奇，想知道究竟發生了什麼事，讓他連穿著打扮都變得不一樣了。以前傑克時常邋裡邋遢，不修邊幅，可是現在他卻穿起乾淨的衣服，還會抹髮膠，有時甚至還偷用爸爸的刮鬍水。爸媽雖然覺得高興，可是總忍不住懷疑為什麼他會在突然間發生這種一百八十度的大轉變。而愛玫則認為反正傑克本來就怪，會做出怪事也沒什麼好大驚小怪的。儘管如此，她還是覺得有什麼事不對勁。

(p.1～p.3)

有一天晚上，愛玫經過客廳時，目睹了一件怪事。她看到傑克一直在打電話，可是卻沒有出聲。他會先撥一組電話號碼，幾秒鐘後，又把話筒摔回去。有一次，他看起來好像真的想講什麼，嘴巴張開，努力想擠出一句話，可是卻半點聲音也發不出來。最後他還是頹喪地放下話筒。同樣的事大概重覆了五遍。愛玫實在按捺不住了。

她問哥哥：「你在做什麼？」

傑克尖叫一聲跳起來。

他說：「妳嚇死我了！我不曉得妳在這裡。」

愛玫又問：「你在打電話給誰？」

傑克緊張得不得了：「沒有哇，我只是在測試電話而已。」

（p.5～p.7）

愛玫才不信，再問了一次：「測試電話？」

傑克說：「嗯……嗯……對啦，我只是想知道電話能不能用而已。」

愛玫緊迫盯人：「騙人，我看到你打電話給別人，然後又把電話給掛了，你該不會是在對誰惡作劇吧？」

傑克大叫：「才沒有！我跟妳說我在測試電話，不管怎麼樣，這都沒妳的事。」

愛玫重覆一遍：「沒我的事？」

傑克說：「對，沒・妳・的・事！」說完，他就走了。

愛玫搖搖頭，傑克真的是愈來愈怪了。

(p.7)

過了幾天，愛玫在洗衣服。她討厭做家事，可是如果她不做，爸媽就不給她零用錢。她捏起傑克臭氣沖天的長褲，卻有東西從口袋裡掉出來，好像是傑克寫的信。愛玫猶豫不決，不知道該不該看那封信。偷看別人的信很不禮貌，但最後她的好奇心戰勝了一切。那不是一封普通的信，而是一封情書，上面寫著：

「親愛的海倫：

或許妳不知道我是誰，我是妳歷史課的同學，我覺得妳是全校最漂亮的女生。我想跟妳說話，可是又怕妳生氣。

神祕的仰慕者」

原來如此，一切真象大白，傑克愛上女生了。愛玫咯咯偷笑著。想到傑克也會愛上別人或交女朋友，她覺得真得很有趣。

愛玫心想：「真想看看海倫是什麼樣子。」

第二天到了學校，愛玫發現原來海倫竟然是嚴校長的女兒。這也正說明了為什麼傑克會怕成這副德行了。嚴校長不喜歡傑克，因為他老是惹麻煩。海倫腦筋好，人長得也不賴。她當然算不上是全校最漂亮的女孩子，不過情人眼裡出西施嘛。

（p.8～p.11）

愛玫決定和哥哥商量，她或許可以幫得上忙。

晚上她來到傑克的門口，敲敲門。

傑克說：「請進。」

看到愛玫走進來，他沒好氣地問：「妳想幹嘛？」

愛玫說：「別那麼兇嘛，我只是想幫你，我知道你在暗戀海倫。」

傑克大吃一驚：「妳說什麼？妳瘋啦？我不曉得妳在說什麼。」

愛玫說：「我看到你寫給她的情書了。」

傑克頓時啞口無言。過了好一會兒，他才說：「好吧，就算我暗戀她又怎麼樣？」

愛玫說：「你需要幫助，我知道你很害怕，因為你根本不懂女孩子，所以我可以給你一些建議。」

傑克承認：「妳說的對，我很怕她和她老爸。前幾天我想打電話給她，可是每次一聽到她的聲音，我就緊張得什麼話都說不出來。」

愛玫說：「她才怕呢，你該跟她說話的。我查出她喜歡古典音樂和莎士比亞，你可以跟她談這個。」

傑克覺得這樣不妥：「我不懂什麼古典音樂或莎士比亞。沒用的，她永遠不會喜歡像我這麼笨的人。」

愛玫笑著說：「並不是所有人都喜歡物以類聚。也許她會覺得你蠢得可愛啊。」

傑克拿起一個枕頭往愛玫身上打。

愛玫討饒：「好啦好啦，你聽我說，我覺得你應該試著和她說話的。最糟的情況頂多是她覺得你是個怪人，然後不理你罷了。」

(p.13～p.17)

愛玫說的對，傑克決定試一試。他知道海倫常待在圖書館裡看書，就從圖書館書架上挑了幾本莎士比亞的劇本，然後向媽媽借了幾張古典音樂的CD。傑克在圖書館找到海倫，便故意在她旁邊的位置坐下來。接著，他把莎士比亞的劇本放在桌上，好讓海倫一眼就可以瞄到。他假裝很用功地在唸書，過了好一會兒，海倫主動開口跟他說話：

「嗨，我注意到你在看莎士比亞，你喜歡他寫的戲劇嗎？」

「噢，對啊，我愛死莎士比亞了，他所有的劇本我都讀過。」傑克在說謊。

海倫問：「那你最喜歡哪一部？」

傑克說：「呃，就是有一對情侶死掉的那部。」

海倫說：「你是說《羅密歐與茱麗葉》。」

傑克說：「對，就是那部，他們被人謀殺了，真教人難過。」

海倫說：「他們不是被謀殺的，是自殺的。」

傑克說：「對啦！我就是那個意思！」海倫回去讀她的書，A計劃失敗了，現在進行B計劃。

（p.18～p.22）

他拿起書包，故意讓幾張CD掉出來。

海倫又注意到了，她說：「你聽巴哈和莫札特，我也是。」

傑克吹牛：「對，我只聽古典音樂，我討厭流行音樂。」他騙人，他只聽流行音樂，他愛死流行音樂了。

海倫卻說：「我也蠻喜歡流行音樂的。那你覺得普契尼怎麼樣？」

傑克說：「對！對！我喜歡普契尼意大利麵。」

海倫噗嗤大笑，引起其他人好奇的目光。

傑克問：「我說了什麼好笑的事嗎？」

海倫說：「普契尼不是意大利麵，他是很有名的作曲家，你吃過法圖契尼意大利麵，就以為普契尼也是意大利麵的名字嗎？」她笑個不停。

傑克氣餒地說：「我就知道。」他的兩個計劃都泡湯，一切都完了。他真心喜歡的女生肯定把他當作宇宙無敵超級大白痴。

(p.23～p.26)

海倫又說：「你從沒聽過古典音樂吧？我也不認為你對莎士比亞懂多少。」

但她並沒有生氣，事實上，她在笑呢。

傑克說：「對，我只是想給妳留下深刻印象，這樣妳才會喜歡我。很抱歉，我要走了。」說完，他站起來準備離開。

海倫說：「不要走，或許我們可以談點別的事啊。」

傑克說：「談些什麼？」

海倫說：「你可以告訴我你和我爸爸是怎麼槓上的。」

傑克很納悶：「妳為什麼會想知道這個？」

海倫略帶羞澀地回答：「因為我相信你的故事一定很有趣……我覺得你這個人蠻有趣的。」

這就是傑克和海倫第一次交談的情形。一直在遠處偷看整件事情始末的愛玫笑了。看來，海倫會是傑克第一個交到的女朋友。

（p.27～p.31）

波波 唸翻天系列

你知道可愛的小兔子也會 "碎碎唸" 嗎？

波波就是這樣。

他將要告訴我們什麼有趣的故事呢？

波波的復活節／波波的西部冒險記／波波上課記

我愛你，波波／波波的下雪天／波波郊遊去

波波打球記／聖誕快樂，波波／波波的萬聖夜

共 9 本，每本均附 CD

國家圖書館出版品預行編目資料

Jack's First Crush:傑克的戀愛初體驗 / Coleen Reddy
著；倪靖, 郜欣, 王平繪；蘇秋華譯. － －初版一刷.
－ －臺北市；三民，2002
　　面；公分--(愛閱雙語叢書. 青春記事簿系列)
中英對照
ISBN 957-14-3658-5　　(平裝)

805

© 　Jack's First Crush
　　　──傑克的戀愛初體驗

著作人　Coleen Reddy
繪　圖　倪靖　郜欣　王平
譯　者　蘇秋華
發行人　劉振強
著作財　三民書局股份有限公司
產權人　臺北市復興北路三八六號
發行所　三民書局股份有限公司
　　　　地址／臺北市復興北路三八六號
　　　　電話／二五〇〇六六〇〇
　　　　郵撥／〇〇〇九九九八──五號
印刷所　三民書局股份有限公司
門市部　復北店／臺北市復興北路三八六號
　　　　重南店／臺北市重慶南路一段六十一號
初版一刷　西元二〇〇二年十一月
編　號　S 85619
定　價　新臺幣參佰伍拾元整
行政院新聞局登記證局版臺業字第〇二〇〇號